DISCOVER 🐾 DOGS WITH
THE AMERICAN CANINE ASSOCIATION

I LIKE
WEIMARANERS!

Linda Bozzo

It is the mission of the American Canine Association (ACA) to provide registered dog owners with the educational support needed for raising, training, showing, and breeding the healthiest pets expected by responsible pet owners throughout the world. Through our activities and services, we encourage and support the dog world in order to promote best-known husbandry standards as well as to ensure that the voice and needs of our customers are quickly and properly addressed.

Our continued support, commitment, and direction are guided by our customers, including veterinary, legal, and legislative advisors. ACA aims to provide the most efficient, cooperative, and courteous service to our customers and strives to set the standard for education and problem solving for all who depend on our services.

For more information, please visit www.acacanines.com, email customerservice@acadogs.com, phone 1-800-651-8332, or write to the American Canine Association at PO Box 121107, Clermont, FL 34712.

Published in 2019 by Enslow Publishing, LLC.
101 W. 23rd Street, Suite 240, New York, NY 10011

Library of Congress Cataloging-in-Publication Data

Names: Bozzo, Linda, author.
Title: I like Weimaraners! / Linda Bozzo.
Description: New York : Enslow Publishing, 2019. | Series: Discover dogs with the American Canine Association | Audience: Grades K-3 | Includes bibliographical references and index.
Identifiers: LCCN 2017051688| ISBN 9780766096875 (library bound) | ISBN 9780766096882 (pbk.) | ISBN 9780766096899 (6 pack)
Subjects: LCSH: Weimaraner (Dog breed)—Juvenile literature.
Classification: LCC SF429.W33 B69 2018 | DDC 636.752—dc23
LC record available at https://lccn.loc.gov/2017051688

Printed in the United States of America

To Our Readers: We have done our best to make sure all websites in this book were active and appropriate when we went to press. However, the author and the publisher have no control over and assume no liability for the material available on those websites or on any websites they may link to. Any comments or suggestions can be sent by email to customerservice@enslow.com.

Photo Credits: Cover, p. 1 Kuznetsov Alexey/Shutterstock.com; p. 3 (left) Dmitry Veryovkin/Shutterstock.com; p. 3 (right) aja H./Shutterstock.com; p. 5 TatyanaPanova/Shutterstock.com; p. 6 Zuzule/Shutterstock.com; p. 9 DragoNika/Shutterstock.com; p. 10 Gail Johnson/Shutterstock.com; pp. 13 (puppy), 19 bitt24/Shutterstock.com; p. 13 (collar) graphicphoto/iStock/Thinkstock, (bed) Luisa Leal Photography/Shutterstock.com, (brush) In-Finity/Shutterstock.com, (food and water bowls) exopixel/Shutterstock.com, (leash, toys) © iStockphoto.com/Liliboas; p. 14 NEstudio/Shutterstock.com; p. 17 Tierfotoagentur/Alamy Stock Photo; p. 18 sdominick/Vetta/Getty Images; p. 21 GaleriaGraphica/Shutterstock.com.

Enslow Publishing
101 W. 23rd Street
Suite 240
New York, NY 10011
USA
enslow.com

CONTENTS

IS A WEIMARANER RIGHT FOR YOU?

Weimaraners (*vie mer ah ners*) are large dogs. They do not do well in small living spaces. If you live in a large home with a fenced yard, a Weimaraner could be right for you.

Weimaraners love to run and hunt.

A DOG OR A PUPPY?

Weimaraners are very smart and have lots of energy. They can be trained to do many things. If you do not have time to train a puppy, you may want an older Weimaraner instead.

Puppies are born with light blue eyes. Over time, they turn light gold, gray, or bluish gray.

LOVING YOUR WEIMARANER

Weimaraners love children and want to spend time with their families. Love your Weimaraner by taking him outdoors for some fun.

This breed is best for an experienced dog owner.

EXERCISE

Weimaraners need a walk on a leash every day. These dogs need to be kept very busy with games such as fetch.

Weimaraners are great to take on long hikes or swimming.

FEEDING YOUR WEIMARANER

Weimaraners can be fed wet or dry dog food. For this breed, two small meals a day are best rather than one big meal. Ask a veterinarian (vet), a doctor for animals, which food is best for your dog and how much to feed her.

Give your Weimaraner fresh, clean water every day.

Remember to keep your dog's food and water dishes clean. Dirty dishes can make a dog sick.

Do not feed your dog people food. It can make her sick.

Your new dog will need:

collar with tag

bed

brush

food and water dishes

leash

toys

The Weimaraner is sometimes called the "gray ghost" because of its gray coat.

GROOMING

Weimaraners shed. This means their hair falls out. Use a soft brush to keep your Weimaraner clean. Bathe when needed. Use a shampoo made specially for dogs.

A Weimaraner's strong nails grow fast and will need to be clipped. A vet or groomer can show you how. Your dog's ears should be cleaned, and his teeth should be brushed by an adult.

WHAT YOU SHOULD KNOW

If not kept busy, Weimaraners can bark a lot and get into trouble. They are smart enough to open fences or crates and steal treats.

Weimaraners are powerful dogs that need strong owners. This breed is not good with other dogs or pets.

You will need to take your new dog to the vet for a checkup. He will need shots, called vaccinations, and yearly checkups to keep him healthy. If you think your dog may be sick or hurt, call your vet.

A GOOD FRIEND

Spend lots of time with your Weimaraner. She will be your happy, loving friend for many years.

A healthy Weimaraner can live ten to thirteen years.

NOTE TO PARENTS

It is important to consider having your dog spayed or neutered when the dog is young. Spaying and neutering are operations that prevent unwanted puppies and can help improve the overall health of your dog.

It is also a good idea to microchip your dog, in case he or she gets lost. A vet will implant a microchip under the skin containing an identification number that can be scanned at a vet's office or animal shelter. The microchip registry is contacted and the company uses the ID number to look up your information from a database.

Some towns require licenses for dogs, so be sure to check with your town clerk.

For more information, speak with a vet.

There are many dogs, young and old, waiting to be adopted from animal shelters and rescue groups.

fetch To go after a toy and bring it back.

groomer A person who bathes and brushes dogs.

leash A chain or strap that attaches to the dog's collar.

shed When dog hair falls out so new hair can grow.

vaccinations Shots that dogs need to stay healthy.

veterinarian (vet) A doctor for animals.

Read About Dogs

Books

Carney, Elizabeth. *Woof! 100 Fun Facts About Dogs*. Washington, DC: National Geographic Children's Books, 2017.

Kenan, Tessa. *I Love Dogs*. Minneapolis, MN: Lerner Publications, 2016.

Stoltman, Joan. *My First Dog*. New York, NY: Gareth Stevens Publishing, 2017.

Websites

American Canine Association Inc., Kids Corner
www.acakids.com
Visit the official website of the American Canine Association.

National Geographic for Kids, Pet Central
kids.nationalgeographic.com/explore/pet-central
Learn more about dogs and other pets at the official site of the National Geographic Society for Kids.

INDEX